the RAIN that FALLS this FAR

ALSO BY DENNIS HINRICHSEN

The Attraction of Heavenly Bodies

the RAIN that FALLS this FAR

poems by
Dennis Hinrichsen

THE GALILEO PRESS LTD
Baltimore, Maryland

Published by The Galileo Press, Ltd.
7215 York Road, Suite 210, Baltimore, MD 21212

Cover art: "Sure Violet," by Helen Frankenthaler. Intaglio on TGL handmade paper, 31½ in. x 43⅜ in. Collection Walker Art Center, Minneapolis, Tyler Graphics Archive 1983. Copyright © Helen Frankenthaler/Tyler Graphics Ltd. 1979.

Cover and text design by Charles Casey Martin.

Publication of this book made possible in part by a grant from the Maryland State Arts Council.

LIBRARY OF CONGRESS CATALOGING-IN-PUBLICATION DATA

Hinrichsen, Dennis
The rain that falls this far / by Dennis Hinrichsen. — 1st ed.
p. cm.
ISBN 0-913123-32-3
I. Title.
PS3558.I546R35 1991
811'.54—dc20 90-3367
CIP

FIRST EDITION

ACKNOWLEDGMENTS

Grateful acknowledgment to the editors of the following magazines in which these poems first appeared:

Agni: "Water Touching Water," "One Wing," "On Trees," and "A Little Music from the House Next Door"

Crazyhorse: "The Straight Natural Blues," "Signatures," "Recurring Sound," "Template," and "Ode"

The Georgia Review: "*The Anatomy of the Crab is Repetitive and Rhythmical*"

Indiana Review: "Unlit Courts"

New England Review & Bread Loaf Quarterly: "Burying a Child"

Poetry: "Testament" and "Poem of Mercy"

Poetry Northwest: "Late Shift," "Against Fate," and "Quadriplegic"

River City: "Stillborn" and "The End of Mercy"

Tar River Poetry: "Free Throws" and "Spectrum"

I also would like to thank the National Endowment for the Arts for a fellowship which aided in the writing of many of these poems, as well as the Michigan Council for the Arts for a generous grant which allowed me to complete the manuscript. The title to the poem, "*The Anatomy of the Crab is Repetitive and Rhythmical,*" is taken from Gregory Bateson's *Mind and Nature: A Necessary Unity*. The quote in the first line of the poem is from *Steps to an Ecology of the Mind*, also by Bateson.

for
Thomas Stutesman, Thomas Mahaffy, Mary Weiner,
and Mary (I've forgotten your last name)
d. May 3, 1968

for
Luci and Sophie

Contents

One

Two

Three

\\\ ONE

Poem Of Mercy

No one poem is enough. No
one poem contains the mercy
I seek, the forgiveness. There are no
words that can approach
the tufts of fine black hair
on the backs of the doctor's hands
as he dialed my home that night
from one of the side rooms,
then choked, looking out into the hallway
at the blood-drenched gurneys,
then handed me the phone
as if to say, "You tell them.
Tell them what you saw. What happened,"
as if only a son could utter
the words that would burn
in a father's ear that night.
Please, a mercy for the doctor.
His courage failed him.
He could not look at me again that night.
And mercy too to the others
who dialed, who fell back
onto their simple faiths, their jobs,
and spoke what few words they knew.
Have mercy: on the dialers, the phones.
Have mercy on the words they used.
And mercy too to the nurses,
the ones who ran down flights
of stairs, only to stare and weep.
Please, a mercy on the quickness
of their gasps. Have mercy too
on the instruments that were used,
what the doctors touched flesh with

and then removed. The coarse towels
and linens. The scalpels, clamps.
The numerous sponges. Have
mercy on the sutures that were never used.
Have mercy too on the light
in the room which was man-made
and all around us in banks.
Have mercy on the detonations
in the bulbs. I think forgiveness
can go this far: to the coffee cup
spiked with pencils, to the navy blue pens,
to the clipboards and spiral notebooks,
to the engraved plastic tags the nurses
and doctors wore like ribbons.
So too to the loose bolt in the rail
on the gurney. To the gurney's one
skewed wheel. Mercy too to the tear
in the mattress, the one
which had become partially untaped
and through which I ran my middle finger
into the matting just to feel it.
Mercy too to the cold medallion they used
to gauge the whip-like action
of the veins in my chest. Mercy
to the pinpoint dots of light.
To the delicate rubber loops
that hung from the suspended bottles.
Even to the dust and bits of windshield glass,
the pieces of the car that had infused me,
a mercy. Mercy to my pant cuffs
and bloodied jacket. To the scissors
because they felt they had to cut away these clothes.
Mercy, therefore, particularly to the scissors.
To the aluminum rods ringed
with curtains, even to the clock
on the wall. My parents finally arriving—

and the curtains yanked—
an opaque sheerness that hid us—
the three of us staring at one another
with the embarrassment of survivors.
Finally, mercy to the bitterness of that sound.

One Wing

Darkness, then, was the dank wool to my nest
of light. I would tip back into
the emptiness beyond my rim of pillows
and let my head drop, my vision weave—

a narrow stalk brushing back and forth
across the ceiling. Then, as now,
I'd sift the risky valence the room's corners held
and guess the direction of the healing drafts

by how alike the cobwebs were to drifting,
skirted fish. And follow then,
behind my head, some imagined line of wind
until my eyelids sank, my eyes finally turned

and rolled. I'd sense then
I'd been taken wholly over—light
to some purer form of light—until the walls sagged
and the manna-breath like coarse rope reeled me back.

It would dawn then. I'd wake and know
that I'd been weeping. It would have been easier
had my hands and feet been tied.
Had I been tube-fed, an IV hovering.

Instead I dreamed—the others' voices thrashing
in the car like birds, the car too small,
and so it floats, a venting cage, above the marsh.
A startled wedge of dusk leaks out. Alights.

Is driven as if by moonlight
into the weeds . . . I wake . . . a row of windows growing

lighter by the moment, a bowl of water redder.
The night nurse combs the shards of glass,

the rough stones. She says, *Calm down, boy.*
It's late. Sleep. It's five a.m. She's the last remaining flaw
in the clearing wash. I'm the one wing
the night chased off to smuggle out

these soul-bits slipped like coins into a glove, a fist.

UNLIT COURTS

to T.M. (1952-1968)

Of all the ridiculous gestures, of all
the self-consoling metaphors
of dust and weeds, the spring lawns
rife with bluebells (and God's
nervy hand among them,
to swat and pluck, to have sway),
I too added a foolishness
as ridiculous and sentimental
as the football field
the size of a board game
they placed on the grass
above our good friend's grave.
What I did was this: I walked out
into the summery brightness
and unthinking, wordless,
drove a wooden golf tee
into the soil above your grave.
I don't know what it meant,
but I drove it down so far
my fingernail took back
a glistening arc of dirt,
part sand, part loam,
and as ephemeral and tasteless
as the phlegm I hawked
into the scrimping wind.
Then I turned and walked away,
back into the city to where
the pickup games were just beginning,
straggling by ones and twos,
accruing toward their complement
of parts—a few of the white kids
lacing up on the railroad ties

terraced beside the river,
some black kids putting moves
on one another with and without
the ball, talking their boastful,
serious, comical trash,
the names we all wanted flung
like swallows into the deepening air—
Norm Van Lier, Jimmy Walker,
and always, at all times,
Earl Monroe—the dark, flamboyant seed
at the core of our imaginings.
How you could enter there
and get caught up . . . The games
would lengthen into dusk,
unspool their loose, miraculous
weaves across the unlit courts.

THE STRAIGHT NATURAL BLUES

A tattery catfish
trolling the last few feet of the river's clarity
like a tube of smoke,
now pitching over, clouded,
like a quart of milk;
or else, in the river's deepest channels, a gar,
a dulcimer grown too fat in the haunches,
stringed by its lateral motion,
its undulations across the currents;
sometimes rising into Picasso's blue shape,
feeding sitar-like on the river's flecked heaven;
or not even this, but river junk, carp,
a soaked log caught in one of the swirling closets;
(bought broke,
then fixed,
then broke again);
leaning like an untoothed saw:
an acoustic Washburn, built Chicago, 1936,
something Huddie Ledbetter or Robert Johnson would have played,
its sound holes jigged like lizards into the chipped wood:
Muse of bruised ivory, of cured pine,
I trash a few notes with a bottleneck . . .

It is 1968 and the hot night air
rifles the vent with its butt end
as Charly Cook and Copper and I
drive ourselves in my father's aqua Mustang
(along with any other black kid from the playground
brash enough to flaunt his moves
and catch a separate ride)
to play a pickup game
against some white kids from another town.

The steaming attic of the gym.
The light going down around us
in gulps, in cubic feet,
as the whole scene grays
and the only thing that glows
is the ball as it caroms
across the windows on the far wall,
our shoe squeaks the sound of some great flock
lifting off, remorseless, blooded
by the warped boards and the porcelain's chill.
The wellsprings of my enduring
good fortune. Paced, when
nothing else would pace me.
Given to the small talk inside the game.

•

In the dream of broken instruments
I am sometimes drunk
a hundred yards below the dam,
listening to the wind cruise,
finally untethered, the river part of town.
Sometimes I am completely lost
in the dream: Joe Bell
sways head and shoulders above
the pitched blade of the water,
sunlight flicking the wave tops,
the insignificant ripplings.
A one-eyed cat mews like a baby
in his blue-black arms . . .
like the distressed tires
cut into the roadbed,
kicking out the low, hard fans of dirt
and stone, the others crying,
pleading really, as if in refrain,

the car chugging slowly through its obverse swerves
like a fish trapped in the miraculous shallows,
the last few feet of the twilit day;
that is, until the blur in the road,
that is, until the pinched shoulder
narrowed to lapsed field,
fell away to marsh,
and the car soared, already bruise
in the bled light, already ghost,
turned and rolled,
already the grass relaying to the roadbed its deepest hurt,
individual and precise, its deepest burn—
the way friends' faces later
would peel away from me,
deflecting my attempts to speak among them:
the whiplash marks of unintended
or intended blame.
Joe Bell knows, the town bum, ragman.
We want this thing in us that is like grief,
that is worse than grief, to pass through us
like a muskrat out of the high grass.
We want it swelled like a wasp
swatted down by the rain,
slaking its thirst
in a miniature pool.
We want the whole muddled thing to flash
the hidden layers of our flesh
and sail—an exhalation
to be picked up and passed
into, out of, another's lungs,
the harsh gear of an accompanying voice . . .

•

I remember once how Copper
bit down so hard on his bitterness

that his lips bled,
and how the rest of us just stood there,
stunned that another player
would chide him "nigger"
to coax a fight
an insignificant winter evening.
And then for days, how that bitterness steeled to hate.
Even years later, when I saw him
at the ARCO, something in him
seethed, something in him flared
from the gas-soaked apron.
Like that night we rode the dankness home
from Paw Paw, our last team loss,
and listened as one of the white kids
bet a black kid he couldn't
jack him off and make him come
and how Copper's face tautened
as his friend's face lowered
into the darkness behind the seat.
What a nail driven through a 2x4
can do to a box guitar—
that's how Bo Diddley played—
his pick the nail,
his right arm the slamming wood.
Copper simply lunged and
slugged the white kid twice.
The back of the bus recoiled
like struck neon, Copper stalking
for the vodka one of us had brought,
taunting pussy this,
what this one skinny white girl could do . . .

I can still see his absolutely perfect
vertical leap as he turns
along the baseline to release his shot,
the almost gentle rippling

like an afterthought to grace;
how he could be said to sometimes
glide, the rock-hard impacts;
how once I ricocheted and cracked
a rib; was lifted then
and pushed downcourt,
Copper knifing into the pack;
how the pain swelled to the left of me
like a slid note . . .
I can still see too Joe Bell's house
pitched like a shoe box
among the weeds,
his pride of strays asleep in the yard;
on the other side of the river, the city's graves,
my own three graves geometrically
placed so that standing, centered,
on the hill among them
I could look back toward Joe Bell's house.
How the bleached walls there cooked
their thousand pounds of grit
and lifted off like talc,
whitening the puddles,
sailing in Joe Bell's wake
as my car stalled and would not start
and the wind picked up as if from beyond the water . . .

what you want boy . . .
better get your ass home . . .

a dust virga raking the river.

Water Touching Water

It's the held, unwavering notes that lure me.
Voices, say, stretched out along the windbreak.
A likeness almost of stillness.
Whistle of a swimmer's breath in a glassy sea.
Grandmother on her slow ride down the jet way,
the canister of oxygen heeling like a mindful child.
My father's father digging with a pocketknife
at his wooden teeth, humming the parts of songs
he knows as if they were one song.
Repeated endings, merged refrains.
His aspirations like warnings almost voiced.
I felt their pressure on me once—
a melisma toward a higher pitch—
as I grazed the painless lacerations,
the webs of dried blood like twisted string.
The auto flattened on the field beside me where I lay.
How memory catches, imperfect as any stretch
of ground, as any fluid body.
The car was like a bullet after having passed
through bone. Companions pinned like underwater blossoms.
Sound of toad creep, frogs. Slur of water touching water.
A hoarseness scurrying, hands and knees, across the razory grass.

WELD

As for the friend glimpsed standing
woozy above the scene
as if above a ruined city
I cannot speak
but let the wind play havoc
and steal—
an unbidden force—
across that night-fed marsh,
rubbing against it
as if against a charm,
erasing smoke and tree,
erasing grass,
peeling back the memory
to its stilled core:
the exposed water's double take,
the mirror's delay:
seeing me he knew
who was still trapped
inside the car . . .

                    Ineffable,
the understanding passed between us:
the arc, then hiss
of a weld:

            him turning
into a buddy's shoulder
as if to fend off time, me
turning in a policeman's
woolen blanket
to grip an armrest
and set my stunned breath pinging

like sleet
across the clipboard
beneath the cruiser's
dented show of light.

for J.M.

Recurring Sound

After 17 years I can still recall
the defining slur the car made as it leaped from the hill's crest
and headed east across the treetops,

slung with tonnage,
a feathery load,
until the engine shuddered once, twice, then whirred

and the car tipped
and the car banked into the reddening curve of dusk.
All that summer its threnody was mine.

The rows of pine
outside my window would wash my sleep,
their soft, protective branches

baffled like owls' wings
to render panic silent,
the small, furious movements and then the glide . . .

In the mornings I'd shoot
basketball or swim. Toward dusk I'd watch the twilight
paint itself across the far end of the lake.

Nothing much happened to me then.
I'd recall the others' stunned faces and the dashlight's glow
and how their faces grew inside it

as luminous as pills.
And I'd recall the tree.
The easy swaying back and forth beneath us,

as if the tree, alone,
could refuse the light
that covered all the other trees like moss

and could ladder down
and cradle
any object drawn like silk across its bark . . .

I remember . . .
                    myself as ghost
among ghosts then, one hand on the dash,

the other in the air, a flame
against my face.
                    I remember, too,

the windshield's curved expanse
and its terms of payback,
hunkered down and holding on, waiting for the car to re-alight.

\\\ TWO

SIGNATURES

Languid seascapes, trams with blurred electric cables,
a pagoda slanting at the pier's end—
this is the record of my father's tour
of the South China Sea, unembellished by his slack face,

his companions' faces, by even the casual leanings
against the squat, gray housings
of the guns. Nineteen-fifty-something. Forty-
nine. A year or two before his marriage. Another six

until his father's death. The way you flick
water to test a skillet's heat—that's the way
my father's memory worked—a few, quick spits,
then hiss, the bitterness accelerates.

We'd sit out beneath the stars and smoke and drink
and it seemed even the night sky
started at his discolorations. Something about the farm
that burned him. Something about a fence.

Here is what he took and what his father gave him:
. . . which is why there are so few photographs and why,
returning, he would not allow himself
the fit of overalls and boots.

Though once, I recall, we drove the county roads,
named for digits, and crossed the bridges,
named for digits, too, and saw
the farm he claimed, the kitchen floor

that caught the afterbirth. Surprised,
the present owners were kind nevertheless

and tried hard to remember his name,
but it was unclear if they remembered. We drove back

the swept, familiar roads.
I don't recall him singing. He hummed, then smoked—
the ditch grass on either side sucked upright by our passing,
the car vents funneling an ever-increasing grit about our feet.

TEMPLATE

Had the doctors only travelled south along his body's axis,
with shears or saw, their hands,
exposed the contents of his slack chest,

they could have parsed for us the pliant tissues.
They could have carried out for later study
a nail's length, a nail's width of heart,

pinched like a dead wire
between the fingers of a gloved hand,
and after careful rumination,

sifting through their recorded facts,
could have calculated back the arc,
the range of instants,

for my uncle's death.
Instead we had to guess.
I picked nearly 4 a.m.

I could feel the mattress
thicken like a field
after having suffered rain

as it claimed his back.
Another chose an hour more toward dawn,
as if to set before us the lure

of ordinary things.
Now he's gone, I have some questions.
Is there wisdom in repeated things?

Did he navigate the fields
by stars as we do now
the stars by earth—

the light at dusk as willowy as ribs,
the portion of the creek we swim,
a heart, incontinent,

all vent? If
he took the time to die that I take
to speak of it,

I'd be sad for him
because he had to face alone the panic
when his chest flinched

and he jackknifed
up and through the pain,
cursing his wife of 30 years,

cursing the butcher's son,
his teen-age daughter, thrashing out
against the loneliness and

misunderstanding that was his marriage, its
keen edge, and how any life's
a hard one,

breath is a bitter recoil—
you rip yourself from sleep and totter as if drunk
among the cattle.

At least, that's what we heard on any given Sunday
of his life, what we
believed, so that newly dead,

he shocked us
with the fallout of his
retreating gaze:

he left behind
his corneas inside a woman's
dimming face.

They prop her up now.
The secret must have loomed like joy. This too
(and what does she describe,

whose happiness is lace,
what she does with stars?
And does his vision, which was simply use,

overlay the current
that is now her sight?): *the cattle tipped*
into the sun like rocks

as if some planet
had been spent, had in fire gone
to seed. And he with just his fingers

adding up to nine, with his pitchfork
and a spade, bucket, limp,
leaning down to put his shoulder into the gate.

Spectrum

The way my mother used to toss chicken in a paper sack to give it that
clown-like powdering
of dust, that drying flour;
the way she shook it twice, clapper in a wooden bell, each piece laid on
the counter in a mockery of flight
or notes, a mockery of love;
she cooked even the gizzards then, though no one ate them; no one cared
about the bony neck and back;
no one even now could remember the simple lights that fed her, the
small vials
she filled with colored water and set across her sill;
how the spectrum moved her, how the colored waters became her
carillon of bells:
shake of the paper sack, Sinatra, bar of yellowed light,
the heart rolled like a glob of spit through dirt, then gently spooned into
the sizzling pan.

Late Shift

They came in waves, those lost instants in the middle of my shift, the middle of summer,
when my lungs reared in the branched darkness and the air around me finally cleared:
it all seemed possible then: the rest of my life, the days like nails to be hammered in,
a ghost-line connecting here and there,
the retrievable past rearing up into the forgivable present like a cycle of rain,
then falling back, and nothing preventing it,
not factory dust and soft fluorescent lighting, the grind of cutters and flexis;
not even the wasp-like buzz of the fans pitched high in the girders could stop it.
I just stood there and let it take me as air can take you, as breath or water.
It was like those nights spent floating in Yokum's pool, as naked as frogs,
as we listened to the semis scream up M-60 just the other side of the trees back of his house
and talked of how crying was useless, prayer useless, the buttery wetness of girls,
and how sometimes the way out was patience, the way in,
though that night the feeling was grounded by Alva Linser peering into the guts of his machine
like a medieval scholar gauging some runic bump in the die, the template—
something for Pepsi that night—
and me just watching, trying to ken what he saw in the oil-splattered gears, his second sight.

QUADRIPLEGIC

I could never touch his pain, though it was always
there before us in the shape of his tools
and the shape he gave to the work. In this way
I was like that house he built once single-handedly,
each day adding new wood to what he had already plotted,
finishing the kitchen first and then a bedroom,
setting the windows tight and wrapping
the rest in plastic so he could live there, teach and work,
each day spent with the smallest fractions of his perfection . . .

•

Not anything I could readily love, but each day
I tried to calm and understand his pain:
how it burned here and there as intense
as a nail driven through the thumb,
a staple just catching a pudge of flesh,
and how he hid it just as quickly
—a cloud flare on a sheen of glass—
as he concentrated on some aspect of my sawing
or how to achieve the proper tension
on a nut and bolt without stripping the threads . . .

•

Which is what happened in a movie
I saw: the aliens grinding each human down
until only the brain and spine were left;
no ganglia of nerves to translate, no coating
of hard muscle to absorb the blows,
just the brain like an overturned pan
and the tail of spine, mockingly prehensile,

floating as pale as a cauliflower among the trees.
And the townspeople running, I don't know why,
the whole thing seemed so tame, just pure thought
suspended in nature, or like puppets of pure thought,
the movie was so bad. And so it failed,
and to chide it, I told him, rambling on until
I saw too late how even the meanest image
could resurrect itself out of the most sterile of pools
and claim living flesh . . .

•

It took him months but he finally told me
it was a black dot that ate him, a cancer
the size of a golf ball, nesting first just off
the spine but growing toward it,
gradually eating in and tearing away
part of the bone and part of the nerve
until the feeling in his arms and legs no longer
echoed with the long, clear notes he knew running,
or coaching track, hammering, sawing,
building his first color television from an elaborate kit;
just stunned flesh finally, barbiturate flesh . . .

•

And dreams of his constant house, which was
eventually taken though eminent domain,
bulldozed through to that compound fracturing
of sticks and unbelievable expulsion
of dust accompanying deconstruction . . . ;
dreams too of the line of firs he called
his windbreak, all of the tools catalogued,
all of the sprays and fertilizers, all of the paints
moved out and loaded in to his new home
so he could lecture the untrained,

teach them nursing, welding, roofing,
the plumb and the square . . .

•

Once, without thinking, I broke a tool
and he just chalked it up, had me line
a row of nails on a piece of scrap as if I were
a schoolboy just learning numbers,
and with minimum wobbling of my line
of sight, with firm grip and unrelenting determination,
had me lift the hammer just below my ear
and strike the nails through . . .

•

You see it was never a pushing through for him,
a hungering toward some foreseeable end or future;
no deep breaths, for instance, following hammering
or heavy shoveling; no sighs
of relaxation, not even when we joked—
just an unrelenting threshold—
as if he were a pane of glass held rigid between the rails,
angling off or letting pass through
the unintended insults of my ease,
the pain like a bullet or rock or wind
just glancing or entering, continually entering
the hidden layers of the glass,
and the glass purpling, reflecting the stress,
but the depth not shattering . . .

TESTAMENT

I understand the viscera, the panic that can seize at any instant the
looped intestines,
or the heart even and its molten core, the fluttery stomach;
it's metaphysics that eludes me,
a dusk-invaded forest, say, and swallows veering, rising out of the
shadows,
slashing with their wing tips the perturbed surface of a lake.
It's all unity, I think, no matter what you know and testaments to its
breaking down, reforming.
Once, when I was 16, a congregation asked me to provide them news of
this,
it was their prayers, they said, that had saved me,
would I describe those barely audible nets flung again and again into
the heavens?,
though I can't imagine how that Sunday would have gone.
The congregation would have first listened quietly, respectfully, to the
young girl
who had just missed making the cheerleading squad, she had practiced
all summer,
and then to her brother and his crippled knee (the men would nod in
sympathy here, then refold their hands), no football, no track,
and how God entered these vacant hearts and swelled them,
and then to me and my tale of woe, how my friends' heads were sheared
clean from their bodies
by some irresistible viciousness, some slashing force,
and how over a span of unrecorded seconds I sat and watched them bleed.
Where could I tell them I saw God? In the marsh landscape rushing
toward us?
The diminishing twilight? In the quick strokes to the backs of their
heads?

Against Fate

To be ripped apart by ghosts, to have no say
in the demons that haunt us,
that choose between one narrow
unpaved road and the next, the constantly

altering parameter of speed;
to have no say in this except with words,
to have such poor shields
as the hands are, the arms outstretched,

as if they were the instruments
of deflection, as if they
could fend off the particles of glass
that memory hurtles out of the darkness

like darts or arrows . . . How else to explain
the panic I felt
on the detour past the washed-out bridge,
the expressway with a section

missing, 80 feet above the river . . .
Even the slow curves there on the bypass
unnerved me, the sunlight
to which I gave an outstretched hand,

knowing it useless against such pressures
as gravity might command,
the incessant, ramming strength of water.
Sixty miles an hour and the highway

missing, you at first sense
a glorious upsurge as of flight, the last remnants

of velocity. And then the weight
of the car takes over. You have time

to sense this. To feel the deft turning
inward, your hands
still on the wheel, the wheel useless,
the landscape expanding at an incredible speed . . .

I keep thinking about the seconds
before the bridge went out
and how those first drivers who made it over
might have sensed it,

might have slowed and tried to flash
their lights to warn the others,
to make them stop, but could only watch
as the bridge turned on its foundations

like a dying beast, and the highway crumbled,
leaving ripped walls on either side
and twisted rebar. How the headlights rose
an instant toward them,

then nosed down
into that terrifying gap . . .
one, maybe, and then another,
before the hopelessness overwhelmed them

and they returned to their still running cars,
the radios on, families waiting,
and felt nothing but disgust and hatred for this life . . .
Knew, too, that later they would praise it.

\\\ THREE

THE ANATOMY OF THE CRAB IS REPETITIVE AND RHYTHMICAL

"It is, like music, repetitive with modulation."
—Gregory Bateson, *Mind and Nature*

"It's all vibrations," Bateson's father said,
explaining how the common zebra's striping

differed from that of Grevy's zebra
and so we might all be pitched like half notes

along this range of sand,
grown to these shuffling half-steps in the bristling coastal air.

I don't hear harmony as I stroll,
but the world's great noise is vast.

Much here is only silence,
encased by gulls at altitude,

by the veer of swallows lower down,
by the vast, great rips

children are renting in the sphere.
If we could hear them, what of these patterns would we know?

What bird engaged with kite engaged
with the clear air closing down,

rapidly closing up the rifts behind them?
The sound we make—leaning down to poke

at weeds, to probe an instrument
the sea has cracked—must be as if we'd tossed

a pocketful of stones into a row
of harps and some of them had fallen—

a day of wrecked pianos at the beach.
Though some kind hand—not God's—

keeps putting things right;
though through all the clanging *wrongs*,

some happiness escapes,
a melody escapes.

"I know of no living matter without form,"
Bateson might have said had he been with us,

laying out into our hands
the crabs he'd seen, limp as kelp—

evidence of his morphologic rhyme—
each segment stitching back

the way it came, though changed,
head to tail through time,

the pattern which connects an aesthetic one.
It is within such beauty we are poised,

wholly risen out of the cell sticks,
out of the musical staffs,

standing by and hauling in on floating strings
the kites shaped like fish, like bats.

A battered entry—kites.
They come back ripped.

The sky everywhere is charged with blue.
Against us, a fine, resilient sand collects.

While some, more brave in love than we,
stroke daylight for the deeper bay,

we all wade in eventually,
casual and intense, to rinse,

each body anchored as it dives into the falling sea
by what the wind deflects:

the trailing splash—
the grace notes—the unfurling plume of wish.

ODE

The kind of rain
I like is the kind
that spills down hard,
that seeks out
deep mines
in the earth's shape
and glides,
wetting down
and drilling
the soft muck.
A process
some men turn
to gain,
siphoning off
that product
of the water's speed
to light
their ever-
flattening paths
and to vent
their rock caves.
This is the string
of all strings
merged,
they might think,
this is the light
that re-enters
like a severed wing
its source—
the underground lakes.
And above them?
Impurities strewn

like stars—sulfur,
igneous rock,
the false gems
and salts
that winnow out, that sift
the water
that seeps back up
the planing tables,
its impurities
spurned,
strums
at an imperfection
in the crust.
The kind
of rain I like
is the kind
that falls this far,
weighted down
by dust.
That enters,
shedding dust,
the deepening lakes.
The panning
as if for gold
that proceeds
without us for us.

On Trees

I have not lived long enough to know
but I would venture
that the trees are friends
because they stay away.
That is to say, this massive oak,
wired together by the city
to keep it from splitting
in our sea-whipped storms,
can calculate without us
the city's fate, the fortune
of the street, can wish
and lie and cheat, can loom,
an undulation, a branching
earth-smeared rib of heaven.
What can it deny?
The mockingbird that flies
stiletto-like from concrete
to its limbs? The sparrows
hopping on its bulging snag
of roots, dragging wings
like Roman shields?
A legion of our area's birds
cuts through the thinnest
of our air, and the air enfolds,
the tree enfolds without
forsaking its buoyant shape.
And yet it's shy.
It hides its tender undersides
of green. Where is the rope
that might raise as from a well
the coolness of its wish?
Where is that contoured branch?

We wear away our shoe soles
on the unyielding streets.
We let our glass doors slam.
The heart is closed, we think.
The massive oak stays put,
serenely courts the cubic
volume of its hold . . .
Toward dawn, the blue jay's screech.
Toward dusk, the insects stuffed
like prayer rags in an ascending wall.

Being In Love

It was on a mortician's examining table
we made love once, having tricked the others

to the sleepy part of day, to become ourselves
in a ray of busted light all hands and

tongues and mist. It was the summer
we made love almost anywhere

as if to test passion's nerve
and so sought out bathroom floors,

attics, porches, an island floating
in the middle of the city in the middle of the day.

Ordinary places but for what we did there,
and the shapes of clouds, and when.

But for the young god who stumbled by
us on the island on his yellow bike.

He was three times blessed—by us;
the drenching sun, his bike; by the story

he could later fashion from the few,
loose facts. I love the way the table

seemed cast aside by unintending hands,
the sections slightly tipped as if to bank

the ancient, recent dead.
Gingerly, so as to not offend,

we put on those idly sifting wings
awhile and hovered in the barn.

I tell this to admit a foolishness:
we were in love. There, and elsewhere—

our bodies' scents unravelling to gather
with the earth-smells, the hair of weeds,

the tinctures hardened varnish makes
when it softens in a press of heat

and fixes to any passing hand which asks,
How far? and Do I stay? and Does passion always

flutter inward before it spills? until—
hair and dust and weeds—it was all one streak,

our small cries of passion notwithstanding.

A Little Music From The House Next Door

The more I wrote them down—
my dreams—the more they roamed and prospered,
as on a guarded night and the moon aloft,

I might hear two wood flutes instead of wind,
and drums, a harp perhaps,
something strung.

How are trees transformed
by dream, alternating spring
with autumn? How,

when I wake, do my dreams revise the fluted
inks of day? I
dream of bombs,

my room's intact;
I imagine dying, and stir
my morning tea. And what of the world's

brilliant work for me? Am I as perfected
as say the sea worm is?
Am I as various and replete?

I suppose I suffer, wondering.
Though argument would count my fingers, toes,
and list them as the local attributes of joy,

the ten and ten of them, my two
eyes combining worlds in equal, patient arcs.
A density of sound, of sight.

A tin can unrolls itself in curving
concrete loops, deposits on the street a trail
of soup. A rank and gloomy

chowder. And what does the alley dream,
transform of place? The strange
and local planet here's in love.

Its nightly products: sperm,
in pints, a kitchen sink
of tears, and rich

emotions flaring the way
the curtains of a house puff once
before a storm, then suck the falling backdrift.

It's quiet now but we can wait.
The alley begins to hide too much if you ask
its dreaming to explain. It's

why, I suppose, the couple next door fighting
is moving toward the couch—
his head between her legs,

or is it hers?—
it doesn't matter. Dream embedded
dream, we get confused. They continue past

the music's romantic ending,
past the final-seeming click as the needle's arm
is put to rest. Past birdsong

on the uncoiling wind. Furious and kind,
obsessed. They have to love this life.
A child playing xylophone could wake them.

Stillborn

I think our voices must have dropped like stones those last days,
like rocks suddenly turned to feathers,
as we called out to him our encouragement and hope, placed our hands
above the swollen tautness . . .

A flurry of drumbeats, perhaps, tailless comets, slurs as innocuous as
those of the blood, quick strokes
in that underwater heaven, goose flesh
in the tepid sea . . .

At least, that's my wish.
I think he must have heard us some, however muted.
I think he must have turned at least once
toward us those last days

before the knot tightened and he shouldered past us
toward different water,
unhurried in his ninth-month robes, no more
delaying,
                    and a different well . . .

(for Steve and Pat Huhn)

BURYING A CHILD

for Joseph Lyle Huhn

Because he is like a doll to them, born into a permanence they
comprehend in stages,
borne on it, in fact, like something dry on the wind,
the children gather and want to touch him; we let them.
Running back and forth on their reconnaissance like thieves through
the slats of a picket fence,
they push through us to trade each new miraculous observation.
A single bear, two squirrels, some unused, windup thing: these toys have
been placed inside the coffin
and seem the real loss to them now, already full-blooded as they are and
tempered to their own currents
of increase and demand.
They wear us out with questions. Why is he so still? His lips so black?
How far into the earth will we set him?
Piece by piece, they give him back to us.

Free Throws

I would concentrate and follow through on each one until I'd shot fifty,
a hundred maybe, it didn't matter—
my arm would swing out straight its endless repetitions and the wrist
would flip
and I would know in the instant that I shot it if the ball was good or not.
In this way I could predict the future, those tens-in-a-row, those
fifteens, twenties, once even forty-two straight;
but it did me no good;
those half-second thrills added up to nothing resembling wisdom or
insight.
All through high school this happened, college, the years of my
marriage,
my wife's pregnancy, my daughter around me on toys.
Four now, she watches me shoot with an air of disbelief yet
compassionate understanding,
asking only that I keep the ball from hitting her when she turns her
back to play with stones.
Such trust: I have to make them all, drawing out those arcs, those
futures,
as rigid as girders, as something curved and faultless spanning the dust.

THE END OF MERCY

Like a slow hiss, I think, the whine a tire makes before it explodes, or
 simply whir of cicada, whir of the window fans.
A sense of fate kicks in then. Or if not fate, then luck, the shape of the
 earth as we go over it,
tensing against the endless miles of road,
saying this part is like a dream, yes, exactly like a dream, this part not,
until our tendons finally preen like stressed wire in the hollows of our
 necks and backs.
Or it is not like this. It is early evening, the daylight falling through the
 locust like a bright mist,
my daughter pitching sand from her log cabin box like water from a
 leaky boat.
It's her life now. Night and not night. I wake breathless in the middle of
 my life.

Dennis Hinrichsen received a B.A. from Western Michigan University in 1974 and an M.F.A. from the University of Iowa in 1976. His awards and achievements include writing fellowships from the National Endowment for the Arts and the Michigan Council for the Arts, as well as the Charles B. Wood Award for Distinguished Writing from *Carolina Quarterly*. In 1983, his first book of poems, *The Attraction of Heavenly Bodies*, was published by Wesleyan University Press. Poems of his have appeared in numerous magazines including *Poetry*, *The Georgia Review*, *New England Review & Bread Loaf Quarterly*, and *Poetry Northwest*. He currently resides in Michigan with his wife and daughter and teaches composition and creative writing at Lansing Community College.

OTHER GALILEO BOOKS

Inventions in a Grieving House, a novella by Patricia Grossman
Days of Summer Gone, poetry by Joe Bolton
The Octopus Who Wanted to Juggle, a children's story by Robert Pack, illustrated by Nancy Willard
Don't Go Back to Sleep, poetry by Sarah Gorham
The Interlude, poetry by D.W. Fenza
Once Out of Nature, poetry by Jim Simmerman
What Happens, poetry by Robert Long
Sandcastle Seahorses, a children's story by Nikia Clark Leopold
Life in the Middle of the Century, two novellas by John Dranow
The Halo of Desire, poetry by Mark Irwin
The Eye That Desires to Look Upward, poetry by Steven Cramer
The Four Wheel Drive Quartet, a fiction by Robert Day
New World Architecture, poetry by Matthew Graham
The Maze, poetry by Mick Fedullo
Keeping Still, Mountain, poetry by John Engman
On My Being Dead and Other Stories, by L.W. Michaelson
The Intelligent Traveler's Guide to Chiribosco, a novella by Jonathan Penner